WIZ

Written by Sally Farrell Odgers

Illustrated by Mark Sofilas

Wiz has something in a box.
Guess what?

A fox!

Wiz has something in a pocket.
Guess what?

A rocket!

Wiz has something in a cup.
Guess what?

A pup!

Wiz has something in a jar.
Guess what?

A star!

Wiz has something in a dish.
Guess what?

A fish!

Wiz has something in a shoe.
Guess what?

A cockatoo!

Wiz has something in a hat.
Guess what?

A cat!
Whoever would have thought of that?